DATE DUE			

The Emperor and the Kite

The Emperor
and the Kite

by JANE YOLEN   illustrated by ED YOUNG

The Putnam & Grosset Group

For my father, who is the king of the kite fliers,
and for my little princess, Heidi Elisabet. J Y

To my mother, "Rivaling the Clouds,"
for her gift of boundless energy and artistic resourcefulness,
and to the friendly rivalry of A.C.S. where it flourished. E Y

Text copyright © 1967 by Jane Yolen. Illustrations copyright © 1967, 1988 by Ed Young.
All rights reserved. This book, or parts thereof, may not be reproduced
in any form without permission in writing from the publisher.
A PaperStar Book, published in 1998 by The Putnam & Grosset Group,
200 Madison Avenue, New York, NY 10016.
PaperStar is a registered trademark of The Putnam Berkley Group, Inc.
The PaperStar logo is a trademark of The Putnam Berkley Group, Inc.
Originally published in 1967 by The World Publishing Company, Cleveland
and New York. New edition published in 1988 by Philomel Books.
Published simultaneously in Canada. Printed in Hong Kong

Library of Congress Cataloging-in-Publication Data
Yolen, Jane.   The emperor and the kite.
Summary: When the emperor is imprisoned in a high tower, his smallest daughter,
whom he has always ignored, uses her kite to save him.
[1. Folklore—China. 2. Fathers and daughters—Folklore.
3. Kites—Folklore] I. Young, Ed, ill.   II. Title.
PZ8.1.Y815Em   1988   398.2'2'0951   [E]   87-18600
ISBN 0-698-11644-5

5   7   9   10   8   6

Once in ancient China there lived a princess who was the fourth daughter of the emperor. She was very tiny. In fact she was so tiny her name was Djeow Seow, which means "the smallest one." And, because she was so tiny, she was not thought very much of—when she was thought of at all.

Her brothers, who were all older and bigger and stronger than she, were thought of all the time. And they were like four rising suns in the eyes of their father. They helped the emperor rule the kingdom and teach the people the ways of peace.

Even her three sisters were all older and bigger and stronger than she. They were like three midnight moons in the eyes of their father. They were the ones who brought food to his table.

But Djeow Seow was like a tiny star in the emperor's sight. She was not even allowed to bring a grain of rice to the meal, so little was she thought of. In fact she was so insignificant, the emperor often forgot he had a fourth daughter at all.

And so, Djeow Seow ate by herself. And she talked to herself.

And she played by herself, which was the loneliest thing of all.
Her favorite toy was a kite of paper and sticks.

Every morning, when the wind came from the east past the rising sun, she
flew her kite. And every evening, when the wind went to the west past the
setting sun, she flew her kite. Her toy was like a flower in the sky.
And it was like a prayer in the wind.

In fact a monk who passed the palace daily made up a poem about her kite.

> *My kite sails upward,*
> *Mounting to the high heavens.*
> *My soul goes on wings.*

But then he was a monk, and given to such thoughts. As for Princess Djeow Seow, she thanked him each day for his prayer. Then she went back to flying her toy.

But all was not peaceful in the
kingdom, just as the wind is not
always peaceful. For the wind can
trouble the waters of a still pond. And there
were evil men plotting against the emperor.

They crept up on him one day when he was alone,
when his four sons were away ruling in the furthermost
parts of the kingdom and his three daughters were down
in the garden. And only Princess Djeow Seow, so tiny she
seemed part of the corner where she sat, saw what happened.

The evil men took the emperor to a tower in the middle of a wide, treeless
plain. The tower had only a single window, with an iron bar across the
center. The plotters sealed the door with bricks and mortar once the emperor
was inside.

Then they rode back to the palace and declared that the emperor was dead.

When his sons and daughters heard this, they all fled to a neighboring kingdom where they spent their time sobbing and sighing. But they did nothing else all day long.

All except Djeow Seow. She was so tiny, the evil men did not notice her at all. And so, she crept to the edge of the wide, treeless plain. And there she built a hut of twigs and branches.

Every day at dawn and again at dark, she would walk across the plain to
the tower. And there she would sail her stick-and-paper kite. To the
kite string she tied a tiny basket filled with rice and poppyseed
cakes, water chestnuts and green tea. The kite pulled
the basket high, high in the air, up as high as the
window in the tower. And, in this way,
she kept her father alive.

So they lived for many days: the emperor in his tower and the princess in a hut near the edge of the plain. The evil men ruled with their cruel, harsh ways, and the people of the country were very sad.

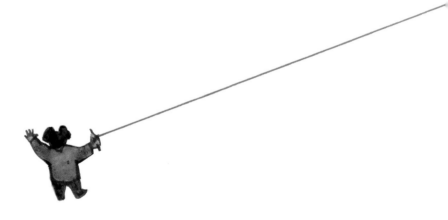

One day as the princess prepared a basket of food for her father, the old monk passed by her hut. She smiled at him, but he seemed not to see her. Yet as he passed, he repeated his prayer in a loud voice. He said:

My kite sails upward,
Mounting to the high heavens.
My emperor goes on wings.

The princess started to thank him. But then she stopped. Something was different. The words were not quite right. "Stop," she called to the monk. But he had already passed by. He was a monk, after all, and did not take part in things of this world.

And then Djeow Seow understood. The monk was telling her something important. And she understood.

Each day after that, when she was not bringing food to her father, Djeow Seow was busy. She twined a string of grass and vines, and wove in strands of her own long black hair. When her rope was as thick as her waist and as high

as the tower, she was ready. She attached the rope to the string of the stick-
and-paper kite, and made her way across the treeless plain. When she
reached the tower, she called to her father. But her voice was as tiny as she,
and her words were lost in the wind.

At last, though, the emperor looked out and saw his daughter flying her kite. He expected the tiny basket of food to sail up to his window as it had done each day. But what should he see but the strand of vines and grass and long black hair. The wind was raging above, holding the kite in its steely grip.

And the princess was below, holding tight to the end of the rope.

Although the emperor had never really understood the worth of his tiniest daughter before, he did now. And he promised himself that if her plan worked she would never again want for anything, though all she had ever wanted was love. Then he leaned farther out of the tower window and grasped the heavy strand. He brought it into his tower room and loosened the string of the kite. He set the kite free, saying, "Go to thy home in the sky, great kite." And the kite flew off toward the heavens.

Then the emperor tied one end of the thick strand to the heavy iron bar across the window, and the other end stretched all the way down to Djeow Seow's tiny hands.

The emperor stepped to the window sill, slipped under the iron bar, saluted the gods, and slid down the rope. His robes billowed out around him like the wings of a bright kite.

When his feet reached the ground, he knelt before his tiny daughter. And he touched the ground before her with his lips. Then he rose and embraced her, and she almost disappeared in his arms.

With his arm encircling her, the emperor said, "Come to thy home with me, loyal child." He lifted the tiny princess to his shoulders and carried her all the way back to the palace.

At the palace, the emperor was greeted by wild and cheering crowds. The people were tired of the evil men, but they had been afraid to act. With the emperor once again to guide them, they threw the plotters into prison.

And when the other sons and daughters of the emperor heard of his return, they left off their sobbing and sighing, and they hurried home to welcome their father. But when they arrived, they were surprised to find Djeow Seow on a tiny throne by their father's side..

To the end of his day, the emperor ruled with Princess Djeow Seow close by.
She never wanted for anything, especially love. And the emperor never again
neglected a person—whether great or small. And, too, it is said that Djeow
Seow ruled after him, as gentle as the wind and, in her loyalty, as unyielding.